GUM
HAS A TU

Val Biro

HODDER AND STOUGHTON
LONDON   SYDNEY   AUCKLAND   TORONTO

ISBN 0 340 33802 4
Copyright © Val Biro 1984   First published 1984   Second impression 1990
Published by Hodder and Stoughton Children's Books, a division of Hodder and Stoughton Ltd,
Mill Road, Dunton Green, Sevenoaks, Kent TN13 2YA
Printed in Great Britain   All rights reserved

'Come on, Gumdrop,' said Mr Oldcastle to his faithful vintage car, 'we shall go for a drive this fine morning!'

He got in and pressed the button, but Gumdrop wouldn't start. He got out and turned the starting-handle, but Gumdrop still refused. He just gurgled and burped. 'Oh dear,' said Mr Oldcastle, 'you seem to have a tummy-ache this morning!'

'I'll give you a push,' said his neighbour the fat Mr Bumblebee, and he leant against Gumdrop. Others came and helped to push too.

The car shot forward and the engine spluttered into life. Black smoke belched from the exhaust and Mr Bumblebee fell flat on his face. And you should have heard the gurgles and burps that Gumdrop made!

'Oh dear,' said Mr Bumblebee as he sat up. 'Gumdrop's got the tummy-ache!'

They were on their way now, with much squeaking from Gumdrop's springs.

'Oh dear,' said Mr Oldcastle, 'your joints are stiff and squeaky too this morning!' To make matters worse it started to rain. Mr Oldcastle drove carefully and he pressed the horn. 'A-tchoooo, a-tchoooo,' it went.

'And now you've caught a cold on top of your tummy-ache,' said Mr Oldcastle in mounting alarm.

Cars and lorries splashed their way past and Gumdrop got covered in mud. Mr Oldcastle could hardly see through the windscreen, so he turned in at a petrol station.

Being splashed and soaked like this could do no good to an old car with a cold.

'Oh dear,' said the attendant, pointing at Gumdrop's thermometer. 'Your car's got a temperature!'

And no wonder, with such a cold and a tummy-ache and squeaky joints, what could you expect? So they gave him some water and Mr Oldcastle decided to take Gumdrop home and put him straight into bed. At least it had stopped raining.

On the way home Gumdrop began to bump and jolt and Mr Oldcastle could hardly keep the steering straight. He noticed that other drivers waved their arms around and kept pointing at the front wheel. So Mr Oldcastle stopped to have a look.

'Oh dear oh dear,' he said in despair. 'Look at that! your tyre is flat! How can I get you home now?'

Just then another car stopped and the children in the back pointed at Gumdrop's mud-spotted sides. 'That car's got the measles,' they said. 'He should be in hospital!'
Certainly he was covered in spots and Mr Oldcastle, in his desperate state, half believed that on top of everything else Gumdrop now had measles, too!

Luckily there was a garage across the road called The Car Hospital, and he drove straight in.

The garage man looked just like a doctor and he examined Gumdrop carefully.

He opened the bonnet, he started the engine, he listened to it through the end of a screwdriver, he poked here and prodded there, he squeezed the tyres, he pressed the horn, all the while making funny little noises like a-ha, hm-hm, tzk-tzk, huh-huh.

'Well,' he said at last, 'Gumdrop is certainly a bit out of sorts today. He has a moderately upset tummy, a slight cold in the horn, a touch of temperature, a little stiffness in his joints and flatulence in his front tyre. And of course the measles. But there is nothing to worry about,' he added with a reassuring smile. 'He will just have to stay here for a few days.'

So they pushed Gumdrop carefully into a nice warm corner of the Hospital. Mr Oldcastle put a heater under the engine and piled rugs and blankets over the bonnet.

Then he patted Gumdrop, asked the doctor to look after him well, and went home.

Next day they put Gumdrop on a ramp and lifted him up. The garage doctor and his assistants were gentle and kind.

They began their work, with spanners and wrenches, greaseguns and oilcans, chargers and wires and hoses and pumps. It was all quite painless and Gumdrop began to feel a lot better.

When Mr Oldcastle came to collect him a few days later, his faithful car was as fit as a fiddle. Even the measles had vanished, as if the spots had been sponged clean away!

And when Mr Oldcastle got in he could have sworn that the engine started even before he pressed the button! Gumdrop was cured and he was impatient to get home.